# The Dementia Garden

*Written by Rebecca Clements*

*Text copyright Rebecca Clements © 2021*

*Illustrated by Gloria Vanessa Nicoli*

*Illustrations Copyright Gloria Vanessa Nicoli © 2021*

*First Edition 2021*

*The Dementia Garden*

*ISBN : 978-1-8382938-2-6*

To Keith, who's garden was always magical.

*L*ily loved to visit her grandfather. His house was cosy and well loved, filled with small trinkets and walls adorned with old family photographs. He always had a big tin of biscuits on the countertop.

*R*acing through the front door, she would often find him drinking tea in his faded, comfy armchair, glasses propped on his nose as he scanned the day's newspapers. Grandpa was old and forgetful, but his chuckle and big smile would always fill the room when Lily entered like a small hurricane, knocking over stacks of mail and old papers.

"LILY! Slow down sweetheart, and give your old grandpa a hug."

Lily climbed up onto his lap and as she buried her head deep into his chest, she smelled his familiar smell of musky soap and toffee.

*L*ately, Lily had gotten to visit her grandpa most days after school as her mother and father checked in on him. He was very forgetful and struggling a bit to remember stuff. Sometimes, he would even forget to finish sentences. Lily didn't mind, she still enjoyed sharing cookies and milk with him and laughing as he pulled funny faces at her and rolled his eyes at her flapping parents.

$O$ne day in late spring, as her mother and father fussed over making Grandpa's dinner and sorting the kitchen, Grandpa and Lily sat together, flicking through an old photo album.

"Who's that?" Lily asked, pointing to a picture of a beautiful lady sitting under a blossom tree. She wore a flowing pink dress, covered in small polka dots.

Grandpa thought very hard for quite a while and then sighed. "I don't remember, dear," he said sadly. "Lily, can I tell you a secret? Well, it's probably best if I show you, actually."

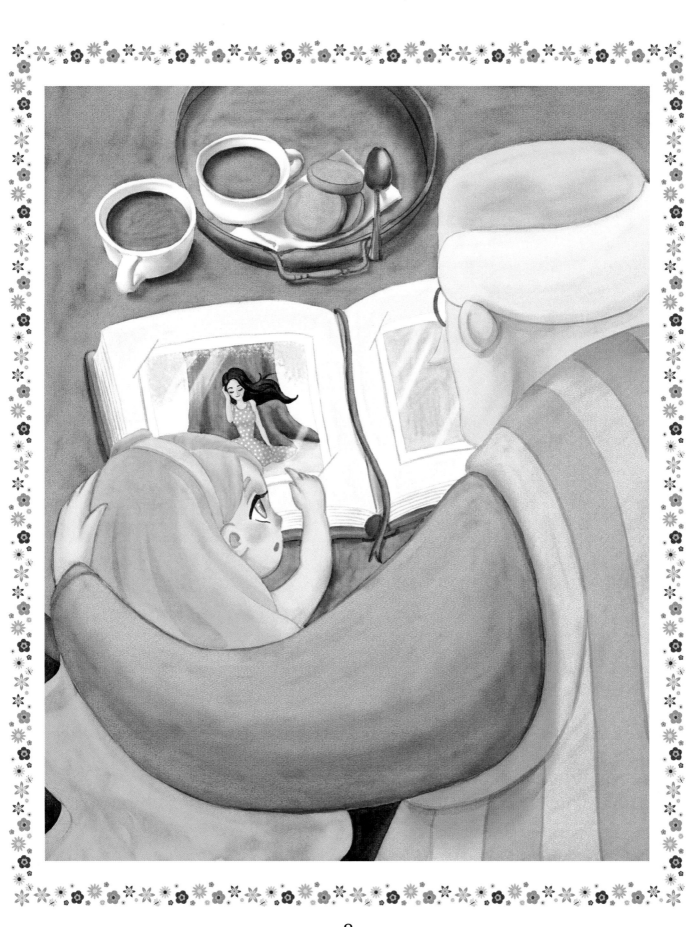

$G$randpa slowly got up and shuffled, in his slippers, over to the cupboard under the stairs. "Come with me."

"Don't you need your walker, Grandpa?" Lily asked, concerned.

"Not where we are going," Grandpa replied with a little smile.

Lily joined Grandpa at the door to the cupboard under the stairs, confused. Grandpa opened it and stepped inside, reaching his hand back to her. Lily checked that her mother and father were still busy in the kitchen and, with only a sliver of hesitation, took his hand and followed her grandfather into the cupboard.

*L*ily gasped loudly. Suddenly, she was standing in front of a large stone wall. There was a big wooden door within the wall with a painted sign that read: **The Dementia Garden**. With a wink, Grandpa turned the old, metal doorknob and pushed the heavy door forward. It gave a loud creak and swung open, welcoming them in.

*T*he smell of freshly mowed grass filled the air, and Lily could hear birds tweeting and children's laughter in the distance. She had stepped into the most wonderful and magical garden her eyes had ever seen. It was filled with huge orange and yellow flowers and big blossom trees. As they walked down the path, they passed a bench with two small children laughing and eating ice-cream. Further along, a dog played catch with a young man, and from a shed came the sound of old jazz music and someone humming along.

"*G*randpa, where are we?" Lily asked, gazing around and trying to take in all the magnificent details. Grandpa, who had sat himself down on a bench overlooking a small brook, gave a very big smile and, with his arms wide open, said, "Welcome to my dementia garden. This garden holds all my very favorite memories, people and words," explained Grandpa. "Let me show you Lily."

*L*ily and Grandpa spent hours discovering all sorts of wonderful things in his garden. They went on an old merry-go-round, ate toffee apples on a pier overlooking the ocean, threw paper boats in the brook and watched them float away, and almost caught a wedding bouquet that came flying towards them amid cheers of joy from a bandstand.

*A*s they walked back to the garden's entrance, Lily saw the beautiful young woman from the photo album sitting under a blossom tree. Up walked a man with a picnic blanket and they both laughed as it caught in the wind and almost blew away. "Look, Grandpa!" Lily said excitedly.

"Ah, yes Lily, that's your wonderful grandmother Annie, as a young lady. We used to picnic under the blossom tree on warm summer days, and those memories I could never forget."

*L*ily didn't want to leave Grandpa's garden — it was such a happy place.

"Can I come back again soon?" she asked as they neared the heavy wooden door.

"I'm afraid not my love. These are my favorite memories; you will get the beauty of a garden with your memories one day. Oh, and Lily? Best not tell your mother and father about this place, eh? Let it be our little secret?"

*L*ily, who was thinking of her favorite things, people and memories to fill her garden (like her special stuffy bunny, unicorn hair clip and giant slabs of chocolate cake), took her grandpa's hand and nodded in agreement.

"Sometimes, Lily, when I forget stuff, it's because they are now stored here and not in my memory. If I get confused with names and people, or simply what I am meant to be doing, it is because I'm in my garden. I could never forget the most special things in my life— they will always be stored here in this truly wonderful, happy and special place."

Leaving the garden, they emerged into Grandpa's hallway in time to hear Lily's mother shout that dinner was ready as they flustered into the hallway.

"Goodness, Dad, you can't walk without your walker," she said sternly and grabbed the old man by his arm, marching him over to his walker. Grandpa winked at Lily.

Over the next few weeks, Grandpa didn't speak as much, and he needed a lot more help with tasks, such as eating and cleaning. Shortly after that, her grandpa couldn't remember who she was, and he even stopped eating his favourite biscuits and toffees. Lily often looked for the grandpa she remembered with such fondness in the cupboard under the stairs, but now the space was filled with old boxes and smelly shoes. One day, Grandpa was gone, and he didn't come back.

Spring turned to summer and summer to autumn and, as Lily played in the park with her mother, she suddenly was showered in blossoms as a gust of wind swept through.

Lily smiled and looked up at the trees, remembering the beauty of her grandpa's dementia garden—the place where he was happily spending all of his time now.

# The End

Made in the USA
Coppell, TX
06 August 2021